D1392012

Cavan Mahony

CLARA
and the MAGIC CIRCLES

Illustrated by Lesley Buckingham

A Making Magic Happen Press Book

Published by MMH Press 2020
Copyright © 2020 Cavan Mahony

National Library of Australia
Cataloguing-in-Publication data:

Clara and the Magic Circles/MMH Press
ISBN: 978-0-6450371-0-4 (hc)
ISBN: 978-0-6450371-3-5 (sc)
ISBN: 978-0-6450371-4-2 (e)

Sarah x

SARAH,
DUCHESS OF YORK

I have truly been inspired by all the incredible children I have met throughout my life, and by being able to experience their imagination and creativity through storytelling and education.

Cavan and I are fellow travellers of miracles and magic. We share our views and visions in order to learn and grow into our authentic selves. I am proud to be part of Cavan's journey to bring the story of Clara and the Magic Circles to life, and truly wish Cavan all the success in the world.

You will meet two daring Irish wolfhounds, Riley and Argus, as well as remarkable woodland messengers – the Robin, Mr. Eagle, Madame Wolf and Miss Butterfly. The irresistible Sir Maheraj will dazzle you. You may just recognize Clara's guide Esmeralda as she walks with Clara through the portals of the magic circles into spellbinding worlds.

Clara and the Magic Circles is a children's book that will enchant audiences of all ages, reminding us of our own heroic journey towards self-acceptance and self-love. Clara's message feels precisely the kind of advice we all need right now, and are looking for, one step at a time, or one paw print at a time!

Of course you have to read this treasure of a book!

"The deepest love of all that lasts forever is the love that you give to yourself."

-Esmeralda

Sarah, Duchess of York

For my husband Stefan and for my son Konstantin.
May you always believe in miracles and know that you are magical.

Opposite: the Author, age 6, with one of her two Irish Wolfhounds, O'Leary

CLARA
AND THE
WOLFHOUNDS

A little girl grew up in a very grand house, and she and her family had a very grand life. Even her Father would play on his grand piano for hours. Clara knew she was very lucky.

Then one day she noticed something had changed at Darlington Manor. There were fewer visitors and parties. The family cook left weary and teary, murmuring something about having to move back home. The piano stood silent, alone, in the grand salon. Life slowed to a cold, hushed rhythm as though only ghosts floated through the big abandoned house.

Clara asked, begged her Mother and Father, to call upon their friends: "Mummy, Daddy, where are Mr. and Mrs. Dingledonger, Suki Larder, and Chas Ching? What about Mr. and Mrs. Clawzing? Why don't they come around any more with their chocolates, little presents and their presence?"

She was deeply dismayed when her parents, Mr. and Mrs. Heart, responded, "Our sweet girl, it's as though we stumbled over a rock, which quite depressed our stocks. Those that came to play unfortunately it seems are not the kind who stay, come what may. We

1

have lost our sparkle and wit and may never quite find it."

Clara's parents went along their days unable to see her ever again in quite the same happy way. Mr. and Mrs. Heart retreated into their studies, making whispered, urgent phone calls. Were they calling about their friends' whereabouts, Clara wondered, or had she done something wrong? Was it her terrible grades in school that had caused this catastrophe? Was it the Nun who said she was destined for hell when Clara misspelled *DUTIFUL* as *DOUBTFUL?*

Clara, distraught and distracted, lay in bed most nights shivering in fear at what would become of her in that lonely house. She stared out the window at the moon, and she prayed for the return of plushy blankets and warm fires lit in the fireplaces and for the sweet sound of her mother singing her to sleep again. She prayed for the sounds of people and parties and for the hustling and bustling. She imagined her Father with his eyes alight, entertaining guests at the grand piano.

As the moon stood silently by, sometimes Clara would sneak out of her room and run down the dark hall in search of a hug from her parents. Yet their bedroom doors were always shut tightly closed, as though there was a big sign that read: Clara Keep Out!

But each day the sun would rise again, and Clara would run downstairs to hug her dogs Riley and Argus, two giant Irish wolfhounds. They were just as cheeky and lively as always. She would walk with Riley and Argus through Britain's spectacular countryside. Clara would climb on the back of one of the wolfhounds when she felt too tired, or just too lazy to walk through the forest that surrounded Darlington Manor. And then, of course, they would play hide and seek for hours. Riley usually won. He was the smartest at making himself as small as possible behind a tree and then darting to the next bush before being caught. Riley and Argus were Clara's best friends. They loved her without a piano or a party.

At the end of the day Clara would return home feeling jubilant and carefree. Her feelings of joy were dashed almost immediately as she walked through the front door, and Riley and Argus were sent away to an entry room.

On one particular day, Clara decided to walk all the way through the house, past the dining room, crossing the great hall, taking a right into the library and then left through the secret bookcase library door, straight into the ballroom. Clara flopped down onto the caramel colored velvet couch and stared, utterly dissatisfied with that empty room. Clara stood up, strode across the room and pushed open the old French doors to breathe in the twilight air and take in the spectacular sight of the setting sun.

Positioned in the middle of the veranda was a wide staircase leading down to a sloping lawn. Two massive stone lions flanked the top of the staircase. Clara pushed herself up onto one of the lions, swung her leg over and her arms around its colossal neck. She laid her head to the side of its mane and felt the setting sun warm her back. As a Leo, born in August, Clara liked to think the lions were made just for her. She half whispered, half giggled, "Hey, have you heard of that song, 'I Am Lion, Hear Me Roar?'"

Clara turned around to the sound of clinking ice, surprised to see her Father stepping out onto the veranda with his evening cocktail.

He appeared God-like to Clara, so tall in his navy suit. Mr. Heart looked pensive, sipping his drink and peering off into the distance.

"Daddy... !"

"Oh hi my little lady, I didn't see you there."

"Daddy, *please*, could you find your sparkle and wit soon so that I can find mine?"

Her Father cleared his throat, "I hope so, Clara. I hope so." It was the first time she noticed creases around his eyes and a strange look of, was it... fear?

And then just like that Mr. Heart brightened. He crouched down next to her and said,

"Clara, I have a plan. Everything is going to be ok. There is a very important man in Egypt I have to see about a very important thing. Your Father is going to build the finest hotel man has ever seen, right on the banks of the Nile! It will be the 8th Wonder of the World!" He hesitated. "We have to leave in the morning. "

"Oh, YES! And then all will return to as it was and I will never be lonely again!" Clara jumped up and clapped her hands. "I will pack my bags right away!"

Mr. Heart gently took her hands in his. "Clara, you must trust me. Your Mother and I have to go to Egypt alone."

"But who's going to look after me?!" Clara exclaimed.

"Two lovely ladies who are really good friends of a friend of a friend. And not one, but two! You lucky girl."

"But I don't understand! What about Bessy, our cook?! Why

can't she come back?"

Mr. Heart cleared his throat again. "These ladies have already agreed to stay at Darlington Manor and look after you. I am sure they will be wonderful – just wonderful!" Mr. Heart said with what distinctly sounded like forced enthusiasm.

The next morning Clara stood in the driveway as her Father lifted suitcases into the boot of the family car. She would replay that moment over and over again in her mind. The crunch of the gravel beneath her feet. The smell of the giant lilac tree just next to the driveway. The dark clouds masking the blue sky. The image of her Mother with her hair pulled back and a soft cashmere coat tied around her waist.

"Clara," Mr. Heart said, "You have met The Ratsibor sisters, Lucinda and Lilith, the fun, lovely ladies here to look after you. I have asked them to take you straight away to your favorite bookstore, Willows, so you can buy one of those silly adventure books you love so much!"

Clara peered over at the two ladies and rolled her eyes. Of course her Father approved of them with all that long wavy hair, the jangly necklaces with shiny medallions and youthful, trendy looks. Lucinda and Lilith looked pretty, she thought as they smiled and nodded. But Clara noted those smiles did not reach their eyes.

"Now, MY daughter is brave and strong." Mr. Heart insisted, "And we will be back in no time at all."

Clara nodded vigorously, staving off the tears that were threatening to fall. She looked up at her Mother who was now holding Mr. Heart's hand. Her Mother looked so thin and tired, as though she might not be able to stand if it were not for her Father's hand. Clara wanted to beg her Mother to stay, to grab hold of her and not let her go, but Clara knew instinctively this was the only way her Mother knew how to fight for the family's survival.

Mr. and Mrs. Heart kissed Clara on her forehead, as though they were just going round the neighbor's house for tea, and then stepped in the car and drove off without a wave of a hand.

"Young laaaaady, get in the car. It's time we get your book," the Ratsibor sisters called from a beat-up grey Volkswagen car. Clara pushed away a creeping feeling of dread and jumped into the backseat of the car. They drove on mostly in silence.

Occasionally Lucinda and Lilith would speak to each other in whispers, necklaces jingling as one gestured, or they would signal to each other in some kind of secret sign language.

Clara smiled broadly as Willows came into view. The old dark red brick building with its windows framed in hunter green felt like Clara's very own magical kingdom. She could see books and books and more books piled high. Clara would spend hours in Willows in a corner devouring *The Chronicles of Narnia: The Lion the Witch and the Wardrobe* or *Anne of Green Gables*.

The car rolled to a stop by the curb outside of Willows. Just as Clara was about to get out of the car, Lucinda turned around to her and said in a slow, menacing voice, "Don't move. We have important things to do first."

The ladies stepped out of the car, slamming their doors shut. Lilith leaned towards the tiny opening in Clara's window pointing a ringed finger at her. "Don't make any trouble."

It felt like time went into slow motion as Clara watched the Ratsibor sisters walk a ways past Willows and enter a large crumbling town house.

Clara shook her head in disbelief. This couldn't actually be happening. Clara tried to open the door but it was locked. She tried all of the doors but they were locked too.

How could she be locked inside a car? She shook the doors as hard as she could and she banged on the windows. Clara yelled for

Lucinda and Lilith until her voice was hoarse. She felt panic rising and taking over her body and her brain. It was hot and she was struggling for air.

And then… everything went black.

Clara sat upright sputtering, soaking wet. Lucinda was an inch from her face holding an empty cup and yelling,

"Wake up, young lady!"

"Did you just throw water on me?!" Clara gasped, realizing she must have fainted from the heat.

"With your antics, it's far too late for any new books! I am going to tell your parents how poorly behaved you are, and oh, what trouble you will be in."

Clara had the sense to keep quiet. She knew she had to get home and call her parents herself, and get rid of these vile 'caretakers'.

Back at Darlington Manor, Clara headed straight for her Father's office in search of his contact details. Clara stopped in her tracks when she heard Lilith say,

"Don't bother. Your Father locked his office before he left. There is no reaching them. Egypt is a long way from England, young lady. We are all you have for now." A cruel smile formed on Lilith's lips.

"Its time we set some new rules. You are not to bother us unless we call for you. Apparently you have dogs at Darlington Manor. We don't like dogs. Keep those wretched creatures away from us and walk them yourself."

"Oh, look at the time! Prepare tea for us and bring it to our wing. Now run along!"

Clara scowled and Lilith laughed. "As the Mad Hatter said, *'What's the matter my Dear, don't care for tea?'*"

Clara spun on her heels heading for the kitchen to prepare tea and whispered, "Just you wait. I will find a way to contact my parents tomorrow and they will return home at once."

Clara woke bleary-eyed from a fitful night's sleep. She had been up most of the night thinking up new names for her 'caretakers' and had finally settled on *The Treacherous Twins*.

Clara sat up, stretched her arms out wide and shook out her unruly hair, realizing she had forgotten to remove a blue hair ribbon. As she glanced out her window, Clara was startled to see their family lawyer, Mr. Brim, coming down the front driveway in his navy blue Range Rover. He stepped out of his car and hesitated, shifting back and forth, nervously adjusting his glasses.

Clara was never particularly fond of Mr. Brim, but in that moment she couldn't have been happier to see him.

Clara jumped out of bed, tossed on her blouse, skirt and trainers from the previous day and scrambled down the stairs shouting, "Mr. Brim, Mr. Brim! Hello there, Mr. Brim!"

Clara pulled open the front door. "Wonderful to see you, Mr. Brim!" Before Clara could say another word, The *Treacherous Twins* were standing right beside her with painted-on smiles.

"Mr. Brim!" Clara insisted, "Won't you come in for breakfast? Lucinda and Lilith were just about to make eggs and marmite soldiers with tea!" Clara stole a side glance at Lilith who was staring unblinking at Mr. Brim.

"Oh thank you, Clara. I would have loved to, really, but I am afraid I have some bad news. You see the British Embassy in Cairo contacted me. It seems your Father was on an official visit to one of Egypt's sacred temples when he suddenly collapsed from a mysterious illness. Mr. Heart has been taken to the best hospital and your Mother is looking after him."

Clara felt the colour drain from her face. She saw smirks of satisfaction coming from both Lucinda and Lilith.

"Can I speak with my parents? Surely they should come home immediately."

"I am afraid not, Clara. Your Mother will contact you as soon as she can, but with this recent event and the time difference and all… I have managed to…. er… hold off the debt collectors for some time due to these extraordinary circumstances. So rest assured, you are safe and secure at Darlington Manor with your charming caretakers. Have faith. I'm sorry, but that's all the news I have to report. I must be going."

Mr. Brim turned abruptly, hurried to his car and sped away down the drive of Darlington Manor.

"Young lady, we will now take *that* breakfast in the sitting room," laughed Lucinda. As the *Treacherous Twins* sauntered off towards the sitting room, Lilith called out; "Don't forget after you've prepared breakfast, make up our rooms and fold the laundry."

The words 'sitting room' resonated in Clara's head clanging louder and louder, until she almost screamed for it to stop… the *FAMILY* sitting room?! *OUR FAMILY* sitting room? *I DON'T THINK SO!*

Clara ran to the side of the house where Riley and Argus were still asleep in their beds. "Quick, wake up! Wake up, Riley and Argus! I need your help!" The wolfhounds stretched their long legs and shook their heads, rising to their full heights. Clara was only a head taller than her dogs. When Riley or Argus stood on two feet resting their front paws on Mr. Heart's shoulders, they stood at over 6 foot tall.

"Riley, Argus, we have intruders in the house. Understand? D A N G E R OUS *intruders!*" The dogs had been well trained and they reacted immediately, barking and growling and showing off enormous fangs.

"Shhhhhhhhh, Riley and Argus. Not yet. Follow me," whispered Clara. "Not a sound until I give the signal."

Clara, Riley and Argus crept through the corridors towards the sound of the Ratsibor sisters' trilling voices. Clara took a deep breath as she stood outside the paneled doors of the family sitting room with her wolfhounds on either side of her.

"Right, ok boys? On the count of three. One…Two…"

"*C L A R AAA, BREAKFAST!!*" shouted Lucinda.

"*THREE…*"

Clara threw open the sitting room doors and Riley and Argus, barking and growling, leapt through with such force, that they tipped over two side tables and a porcelain vase came crashing to the floor.

Lucinda and Lilith jolted up and off the couches screaming like lunatics. They ran every which way looking for cover behind any big piece of furniture. Riley and Argus vaulted over chairs and couches snarling as they went until the wolfhounds had pinned the *Treacherous Twins* into a corner.

"Riley, Argus, sit, heel!" Clara commanded. The dogs immediately calmed and sat guarding their 'intruders.'

"Lucinda and Lilith, we are indeed setting some new rules. At my command at any time, Riley and Argus will attack you and tear you to pieces. You are to stay in the assigned wing, out of my way, and far away from me. You are not to set foot in this part of the house."

Clara stood as tall as she could and raised her voice, "*HAVE I MADE MYSELF CLEAR?!*"

The ladies nodded simultaneously. They were both visibly shaking from fright.

Clara called to her wolfhounds, "Riley, Argus, come to me now." The wolfhounds moved over to Clara but they did not sit down. Instead they flanked Clara and glared at the Ratsibor sisters

Clara pointed, "Now Y O U, *LEAVE ME ALONE!*"

Lucinda and Lilith scurried past them as Riley and Argus barked and growled. Clara heard them both running away down the hall, necklaces jangling all the way.

Clara felt such euphoria, she shouted, "YES! We won! We won!" Overwhelmed with relief, Clara dropped down on the soft carpet and hugged her dogs. As Clara considered her victory, it began to dawn on her just how alone she really was in her own home.

Was her Father going to get better? *When* would her parents come home? *Would* her parents *ever* come home? *Would she be lonely forever more?* Waves of grief washed over Clara until she was sobbing uncontrollably.

After a time, Clara had calmed herself down to an occasional hiccup. "Riley, Argus, shall we forget everything just for now and go play in our forest?" The wolfhounds barked in agreement.

C lara, Riley and Argus reached the usual clearing in their forest. Still shaken but determined to forget about the *Treacherous Twins* for a while, Clara jumped straight into their favorite game of hide and seek.

As they bounded about, suddenly a beautiful lady with a hat perched on her long red hair, and a green cape draped over her shoulders appeared in the clearing. The lady carried a velvet pouch that jangled merrily as she walked.

Clara, Riley and Argus, surprised to see anyone, stopped what they were doing, and Clara said, "Well hello there. May I ask where are you going?" The beautiful lady replied: "Oh, today I am going everywhere, and nowhere, of course. And you? Where are YOU going?"

Clara, rather confused by the lady, stuttered, "I, I am here. I am not going anywhere."

"Oh what fun!" Answered the beautiful lady. "I'm here too! What's so important about going anywhere? It's only right now and right here that matters. Allow me to introduce myself. My name is Esmeralda."

"Oh, how do you do. My name is Clara, and these are my best

friends, Riley and Argus. We were just playing a game. Would you like to join us?"

Esmeralda smiled. "Oh I do love feeling like playing a game."

Clara, perplexed by Esmeralda's answer, was about to ask her if that meant she would actually join their game, when Esmeralda continued,

"I see you have lovely friends. Do your parents mind you being out here in the forest?"

"Oh, I'm afraid my parents lost their sparkle and their wit and my Father went to go look for it in a far away place and fell ill," choked Clara. "I try to feel better out here in our forest with Riley and Argus amongst the trees, instead of lonely at home."

"Ah, I see," Esmeralda said. "Did you know that anything your heart desires, if you can imagine it, you can create it! I carry this bag with me for occasions such as these – when it's time for a great adventure."

Clara studied Esmeralda for a moment and felt emotions welling up inside of her. Sadness, anger and frustration tangled knotting together in her stomach.

This is no time for a great adventure, Clara thought.

Esmeralda reached into her velvet bag and pulled out a handful of –GASP- the brightest and most sparkling stones Clara had ever seen. Not even the ladies who came to their parties with their shiny rings and bracelets of diamonds, sapphires and rubies could match what danced before Clara.

Every colour imaginable… green, purple, blue and white, violet and amber twinkled and shimmered. Clara wondered if she was imagining the faint glowing circles that surrounded each of the gems. Riley and Argus barked and sniffed, wagging tails, sensing this was something very important.

"Now," Esmeralda said, "you can pick four gems, one at a time, and each one will take us on an adventure to an enchanted land."

Clara suddenly felt a fizz of excitement. Going to a magical place?! Perhaps an adventure was just what she needed after all. Clara smiled for the first time in what felt like a long, long while.

Clara was about to reach for a sparkling stone when Esmeralda exclaimed,

"Oh! Did I mention sparkle and wit are the main ingredients for a birthday party? Perhaps the only sparkle and wit that you need is your own.

So let's begin, shall we? Clara, reach for the gem that calls to you the most."

THE EMERALD AND THE ROBIN

Clara immediately picked out a giant green gem from Esmeralda's hand. "Ah, that's wonderful Clara. You have chosen the Emerald, my namesake! The Passage of the Emerald will teach you about the nature of true friendship and also of hope and new beginnings."

"In order for this to work, you must do exactly as I say. Hold the Emerald out in front of you with your left hand. Place your right hand on your heart. Close your eyes. Imagine all that makes you happy and that you appreciate, and feel it in your heart."

Clara gripped the Emerald and squeezed her eyes shut as she shouted out: "Riley and Argus, birthday cake, lilies, the sound of the piano playing, the wind blowing in the trees, hugs and kisses from my parents, satin and silk dressing gowns, my teddy bear…"

Clara suddenly felt so happy, she burst out: "Thank you! Thank you! Oh, Thank you!"

Esmeralda said, "Yes, you've done it Clara! Now open your eyes to the Passage of the Emerald!"

Right there, in front of Clara, were three huge circular rings of green light, glowing and pulsating. The giant green circles cast a light so bright that all the forest surroundings took on the same electric emerald hue.

Noting Clara's surprise and trepidation, Esmeralda exclaimed, "Oh, come on then! It's not every day one gets to walk through an emerald portal into an enchanted world!"

Clara looked at Riley and Argus standing tall on either side of her. They seemed to nod their approval. Together they followed Esmeralda through the shimmering green circles, and there, on the other side, was...

Exactly the same forest! "What is this?!" Clara exclaimed, "We are in the very same forest, the very same clearing. There is nothing new and magical here from that Emerald you hold so dear!"

"What makes you so sure Clara? Open your heart and your eyes will see what is truly before you. Walk with me."

Clara, Riley and Argus wandered along the winding forest path with Esmeralda until they came upon an old stone footbridge covering a stream. The stream gently gurgled along underneath their feet. The water glistened and sparkled in the sun as it bounced off rocks and made its way downstream.

The wind blew through the birch trees, rustling branches and ruffling leaves. Clara leaned over the side of the bridge, mesmerized by the swirling, twirling movements of the stream. As she studied the water, tall stems of swaying pink flowers caught her attention.

"Oh, don't they look like tall elegant pink ladies, Riley and Argus?" The stems on the banks of the stream were beckoning her closer. Their pink bulbs were just the very size of her fingers. "I could put all those pink bulbs on my fingers and it would be like having ten new friends for my ten fingers!"

Clara was so engrossed in her thoughts that she didn't hear the flutter of tiny wings right by her ear. Then suddenly sensing someone or something trying to get her attention, Clara looked over at her left shoulder. And there, sitting as calm as a cucumber, was a robin.

Clara dared not move or breathe. She had never been this close to a robin before. They were normally far too frightened of her.

Strangely, Riley and Argus didn't bark or jump up. They simply bowed their heads and lay down next to her on the bridge. With big questioning eyes, Clara looked at Esmeralda.

Smiling, Esmeralda said: "Listen to the Robin's song, and it will speak to you, Clara." And with that, Esmeralda turned, and wandered away deeper into the forest.

Clara very carefully and very softly said, "Dear Robin. You are beautiful! Will you come and sit in the palm of my hand and sing to me?" To Clara's great surprise the Robin flew up and landed on her outstretched hand. It puffed out its orange-reddish chest, opened its little beak, and out came the most beautiful, happy, jubilant, sing-song robin song.

And then the most extraordinary thing happened. The Robin cocked its head to the side and said, "Dearest Clara, always carry your own song in your heart! Sing it everywhere, and fill the skies with your song. You will find happiness where there was none. A frown will become a smile, and you will always be surrounded with the people who can hear your heart song."

"Oh thank you little Robin. That must mean, if I sing our friends' favorite song, they will all come back to play!"

"They may come back to play, but it is only when you sing the song that comes from your own heart, that you will know the difference between a true friend and a false friend."

Instinctively, Clara looked over at the stems of pink flowers she wanted so much to befriend a moment ago. They were no longer swaying playfully. They stood stock still together, like an army readying for battle.

"The Foxgloves," said the Robin, "Are just those false friends. They are beautiful to look at, yet they are full of poison. In this land, had you played with the Foxgloves, they would have pulled out your energy and eventually siphoned off your life source."

"Oh dear," said Clara, "Who needs friends like these?! But what if no one likes my heart song and I will be lonely forever more? I wish for my Mother to sing her heart song again."

The Robin answered: "Look at how small I am, and yet my song is mighty. I am so happy singing my heart song on my own, and yet I am not alone. Don't be afraid to fill the skies with your song. When the melody bursts forth from your heart, you will feel a joy that triumphs over any doubt. When you sing from your heart, true friends will hear it and they will come to sing it with you. Sing your song, Clara, and eventually you will hear your Mother sing hers again too!"

"I will watch over you now, and come visit you in your garden every day to remind you that you have a song to sing, and that you are never alone!"

Clara felt her heart expanding. She could feel it grow so large that she thought it might burst.

"I know that Riley and Argus are my friends! And now I know that you are my friend! And I can't wait to meet more friends, just as special as you are, little Robin."

The Robin proudly puffed out its chest: "This is just the beginning, Clara, of a great adventure. Esmeralda is waiting for you in the next clearing!" And in a moment, the Robin fluttered up into the blue sky and flew on its way.

THE RUBY AND THE EAGLE

C lara waved, "See you soon, my friend! Come on, Riley, Argus, let's go find Esmeralda." Clara and the two wolfhounds skipped their way over the bridge, deeper into the forest. As the path narrowed, they walked single file through the trees. Clara breathed in the smell of wild garlic and brushed her hands along the rows of its white flowers. She listened to the cacophony of all the different bird sounds. Each one singing is its own heart song, she thought!

The path widened and opened into a new part of the forest full of giant gnarled trees, with branches covered in brilliant, chartreuse-coloured moss. Clara found Esmeralda lying back in the nook of one of these grand, old trees, whistling a happy tune.

"Are you ready for another adventure Clara?"

"Oh why, yes! Please!"

Clara noticed for the first time little colorful sparks firing out of Esmeralda's velvet bag. Clara eagerly reached into Esmeralda's bag and pulled out the darkest, deepest, fiery red gem.

Esmeralda smiled knowingly, and said, "Now, Clara, you will experience the Passage of the Ruby. The Ruby will teach you about courage, about vision and about the meaning of purpose."

"I'm rather small for a purpose," thought Clara, "Well, here goes!"

Clara placed her right hand on her heart, held the Ruby tight in her left hand and closed her eyes. This time she thought about the Robin's song. Clara saw herself singing, arms outstretched to the sky. Clara imagined another girl with a big smile who heard Clara's heart song and came to sing along with her. And then Esmeralda said,

"It's time, Clara." Clara opened her eyes, and before her were the massive pulsating glowing circles, but this time they were deep red. The forest around Clara was now bathed in ruby-red from the light of the circles.

Clara braced herself and Riley and Argus flanked her on either side. They followed Esmeralda into the ruby-red circles.

On the other side, Esmeralda beckoned them deeper into the mossy forest. "You have quite a climb ahead of you now, Clara. Keep going until you reach the old Roman beacon. You will know when you have reached your destination. Now, jolly ho! Off you go!"

Clara looked up at those great big hills and remembered she had never been keen on up-hill walking with all that huffing and puffing. But when Clara spun around to have a good talking to with Esmeralda, she had vanished!

"Oh, bother!" Clara stomped. "Riley, Argus, it seems there is only one way out of here, and it's up!" The wolfhounds immediately moved up ahead on the path. Riley and Argus stopped, looked back and barked, urging Clara forward. Clara furrowed her brow in determination, and off they went.

Clara and the wolfhounds walked up, and up, and up. They picked their way through brambles and thistles and all sorts of bristles. They scrambled over fallen trees and piles of rocks. Her breathing became ragged. Her legs ached. She didn't like this magical Ruby world one bit.

Just as she was about to give up, Riley and Argus crested the hill and disappeared. Clara heard happy barking and she knew they had reached the top.

"Oh, finally! This is it!" Clara exclaimed. "I bet this magical Roman beacon will be made of gold! And there will be a swing set, and, oh, a giant table full of scones and cream and pudding and strawberry tart and chocolate cake!" Suddenly full of energy, Clara shot up the last steep bit to arrive at an expansive flat hilltop to see…

A 20-foot high rusty old structure that resembled something like a giant spikey torch, with nothing else but green grass as far as the eye could see.

Riley and Argus couldn't believe their luck finding themselves in a place of open terrain. They galloped freely around the perimeter, and back and forth across the field.

"**ES MER AL DAAAAA**!!! I am tired of this silly old trick! I am angry! I am going to shout and scream and jump up and down if you don't come out right now, because *I AM HUNGRY!!*"

"Hmmmm, and I am hungry too," came a deep rasping voice. Clara stopped still. The hairs on her neck prickled. She looked up in the direction from whence the voice came and there, perched high atop one of the iron spikes of that Roman beacon, was an enormous eagle.

Trying not to show her shock at this unusual encounter, Clara said, "Uh, hello Mr. Eagle! Did you say something?"

The great eagle shook his back, momentarily expanding his giant wings as he did.

"Yes, I did. I was just thinking about catching my next meal." His big yellow eyes glinted in the sunlight.

Clara cast her gaze around to see if her trusty dogs were nearby to come to her rescue, but, alas, they had both fallen asleep in the grass after all that galloping about.

"Are you afraid of me?" whispered the eagle. Clara thought, I will simply keep up a polite conversation, and responded, "Of you? No. Although I suppose, I am afraid of the dark."

"Maybe you should be afraid of the light, too," said the eagle, bending his head and beak forward and down menacingly.

Clara felt a sticky, sickly, dizzying sensation starting in her head and coursing down to her stomach. Soon it would take over her whole body and her legs would no longer keep her upright.

"OK, enough!" She said to herself. "In horse riding, I learned animals smell fear, and then it all goes horribly wrong. So trying to run away in fright on this open field certainly isn't going to work. How do I face a bully? Stand up to IT! So that's it. I know what to do. I am TOO BIG for this bird!"

Clara put her shoulders back, jutted her chin forward and squared up directly to the spike and pointed at the eagle.

"Beware, Eagle, when the hunted becomes the Hunter. I am not afraid of you.

I am quick and I am nimble. I am smarter than you, and my thoughts are arrows. I don't believe in hurting anything, but if you come near me, I will capture you. And I will make eagle stew out of YOU!"

The eagle considered this. Suddenly he let out a chortle. He found he respected this strange oversized small creature. Perhaps she was more like the eagle than he thought.

"Do you know why eagles have great strength and power?" he asked.

"No I don't think I do," said Clara.

"We have vision and we have courage. Look around you. I have a 360-degree view of all the valleys below. I wait. I observe. Then I fly. Then I hunt. Eagles are courageous because we do not fear storms like other birds and animals. We know that the way to survive the storm is to fly above it."

"Thousands of years ago the Romans would light this beacon I am resting on, and others located on different hilltops, to make fiery torches in the sky, to warn surrounding villages of an impending enemy attack. The Romans, like the eagle, had the vision from the hilltop to observe the world below. You have shown determination to climb these hills, and courage to stand up to me. Now you know to have vision to step back and look before you act."

"You have a friend in me now, for life," said the eagle. "Know that I can see you from far, far away as I swoop over your home. And when you look up and see me, you might notice a ruby red glow around my wings and you will remember to be brave, and know that you can weather any storm."

With that, the mighty eagle flapped his great wings and lifted off from the Roman beacon, quickly rising until he was soaring far, far above in the sky.

Clara leapt into the air for joy. "I did it! I am strong! I can take care of myself. And I have another friend in the eagle! Good-bye Mr. Eagle!"

Clara was just remembering that she was very, very hungry, when she saw Esmeralda waving at her from a distance. Riley and Argus had already found Esmeralda. Wagging their tails and snorting with delight, the wolfhounds disappeared over the hill with her.

"Wait for me!" shouted Clara as she ran after them. She stumbled over the side and tumbled down a long grassy sloping hill, skidding to a stop just before catching a glimpse of Esmeralda, Riley and Argus disappearing into a tall thicket of leafy trees at the bottom.

Clara, feeling quite proud of herself for standing up to Mr. Eagle, stood up, brushed herself off and marched straight into the that thicket of...

TREES!! Glorious trees that bowed to one another, forming a great big canopy of out-stretched branches and leaves. Clara thought it looked like a lovely marquee made of bark and twinkling, fluttering leaves.

And under that great marquee of branches and leaves sat Esmeralda behind a long wooden table. One golden ballroom chair stood unoccupied with a snuggly, soft blanket hanging over its back.

Clara stared in disbelief at the feast before her. Towers of cucumber and egg sandwiches, crackers and biscuits. There were cakes covered in white icing with strawberries and cupcakes with pink icing and rainbow sprinkles. Chocolate brownies with fudge sauce sat right next to bowls of steaming hot scones. There were apple and custard tarts mixed up with crunchy meringue. And if that wasn't enough, it was all arranged upon china plates painted with lily pads. The china teapot and the teacups with scalloped edges and painted jumping frogs rested on a gleaming silver tray at the end of the table.

"Oh, Esmeralda!" Clara clapped her hands together in excitement, "This is the MOST *scrumptious, deluncious, fantastical* tea I have ever seen!" And with that Clara lunged straight for the pink cupcakes.

Esmeralda put up her hand. "Ah, ah! Manners, young lady! Manners! Please take your seat at the table." Clara pulled herself together and tried to sit down in the most ladylike fashion she could imagine.

"Clara, what do you think comes next?" Clara thought about it, and said, "Yes! Of course! We are meant to start with the cucumber and egg sandwiches first, not the cupcakes! Silly me."

"No," responded Esmeralda, "We give thanks first for the food we are about to eat. And why do we do that, Clara?"

Clara couldn't help it. She was so hungry and so tired. She rolled her eyes and sighed, "Oh right, I suppose it's polite to thank our lucky stars for the food we are about to eat."

With a big smile Esmeralda said, "When we SAY thank you for our food, or for the wind in the trees, or the stars in the sky, we FEEL thankful. And when we feel thankful, that's when the real magic happens. Don't you remember?"

"Like the Emerald, or the Ruby passage!" Clara nearly shouted.

Clara closed her eyes, and put her hand on her heart. She said, "Thank you! Thank you Riley and Argus! Thank you, Esmeralda! Thank you for this delicious food!" And she could actually taste the sandwiches and the scones and the cakes without even having touched one.

And just like that, Clara suddenly had her own big plate full of scrumptious treats and a china cup of sweet-smelling tea. She touched the headband of wildflowers and ribbons that had appeared on her head. She laughed out loud at Riley and Argus' bowls that were now full of sausages.

After Clara had sampled every treat, she considered a moment, and said to Esmeralda, "I now know something of courage, and of vision. And I think I understand the meaning of purpose. You are sharing magic, adventures, and joy with me. That must be your purpose in life and there could be no greater purpose! From now on, it will be my purpose too!"

"Clara, you have completed the Passage of the Ruby. We must go! No time to waste." Clara reached for one last sip of tea and was surprised to see the painted frog missing from her cup.

"The frog jumped to the saucer's lily pad, of course!" Esmeralda laughed.

THE DIAMOND AND THE WOLF

Dusk had fallen over the valley. Pink clouds dotted the evening sky. Esmeralda held out her velvet bag and Clara reached in and pulled out what looked like a crystal with a flashing prism of white light.

"You have chosen the diamond, Clara. The Passage of the Diamond will teach you about inner strength, freedom, and faith."

Clara couldn't help but smile. A real diamond, she thought. Surely this will be fun!

Hand on heart, and clutching the diamond, Clara closed her eyes and thought about her friends the Robin and the Eagle, and about Esmeralda, Riley and Argus. She was so bursting with love that she knew she didn't even need Esmeralda to tell her to open her eyes.

There, in front of Clara, were the giant, pulsing circles in white. "I imagine Heaven would be this colour," said Clara looking around at her now glowing, bright white surroundings. And together they all walked into the white Diamond circles.

The sun was disappearing below the horizon. Clara felt the familiar sticky, sickly sensation in her stomach knowing that nighttime was approaching. The feeling was quickly replaced by elation when she discovered there was a whole area arranged around a warm, burning firepit with brightly colored woven rugs and lots and lots of squishy pillows. Lanterns big and small were dotted around, glowing with flickering candle light. She was about to flop down on the rugs when Esmeralda picked up one of the lanterns and handed it to Clara.

"You will need this to light the way on your journey. Don't worrrry!" Esmeralda said seeing Clara's surprise, "It's not heavy. You can carry it for miles!"

"I-I am afraid of the dark." stammered Clara. "I can't walk by myself with Riley and Argus, without you!" Esmeralda embraced Clara in a big hug and whispered in her ear, "You are never alone, Clara. I am with you in your heart. Trust in the Passage of the Diamond. "

Esmeralda released Clara and looked directly into her eyes. "You know of courage. Go!" Signaling the end of the discussion, Esmeralda moved away to take her place by the fire.

Clara took a deep breath, gripped the handle of the lantern, turned and walked straight ahead into the darkening forest, with Riley and Argus following behind. The darkness settled in around her. Clara noticed the changing rhythm of the forest. There were nocturnal bird sounds like the hooting of the owl in the distance, "*Hooooo hoooooo.*" The roots and leaves seemed to crunch louder under her feet as she walked. Low bushes and ferns rustled and quaked, as little animals scuttered through them.

"I am not afraid of the dark. I am not afraid of the dark. I am not afraid of the dark!" Clara repeated to herself, over and over again.

Clara wondered what she was looking for this time and how she would know when she found it. The trees began to thin out and the terrain grew rockier and more open. She discovered that she no longer needed the lantern to light the way.

Clara came upon a configuration of several large boulders that had been worn smooth and flat by centuries of weathering. She stopped, put the lantern down and looked up at the night sky and exclaimed, "Riley, Argus, look at the full MOON! That's why we no longer need this lantern! Our moon has lit up the entire night sky and all the land before us!"

Riley and Argus were busy drinking from the stream nearby. They simply wagged their tails in acknowledgement.

"I think this is as good a place as any to take a rest. Shall we?" Riley and Argus jogged back to her and lay down on the low rocks.

Clara scrambled up to the highest rock, sat down and hugged her knees to her chest. She cast her eyes up to the bright, glowing moon. She felt peaceful. "This isn't scary at all," she said to herself. "The moon is my friend. Sitting under the moonlight is so much better than looking at it from my bedroom window."

Clara yawned and relaxed in that delicious way. "Oh," she giggled. "Wouldn't it be nice if in this Diamond magical world there were a gallant Knight here to bid me good night!" And with that, Clara drifted off to sleep.

Clara was startled awake by a single, wild, mournful howl, "Awoooooooooo!!" It was silent for a moment and then again louder still, "Awoooooooo!!" Clara peered out into the distance and inhaled sharply seeing a wolf with its head up to the night sky howling at the moon. Without thinking, Clara jumped up to a standing position on her rock.

The wolf must have heard her, or smelled her, or felt her presence. Its head snapped down and sideways so that the wolf stared straight in Clara's direction. Then it began to move towards her. She could see its purposeful steps and as it came closer, the moon illuminated the muscles and hackles bristling on its back. Its ears stood straight up, its eyes penetrating her very soul.

The wolf stopped below Clara, just short of her rock, and growled, "This is my territory. This is my land. That is my rock. Everything here belongs to me. And you are not welcome!"

Clara standing above, looking down from her rock, thought of Mr. Eagle, of courage and of vision. This wolf too would surely respect courage, and become her friend. Clara put her hands on her hips, and made her self as large as possible and leaned forward.

"Madame Wolf, I am not afraid of you. I go where I please, and it pleases me to be here now. I have as much a right to this terrain as you do. If you try to attack me, I will punch you in the nose and my two giant wolfhounds will swat you off this rock – and you will never howl at the moon again!" Clara emphasized this statement with a stomp, and a vigorous nod of her head and her fiercest frown.

With eyes full of menace and lips curled back exposing her sharp fangs, Madame Wolf hissed, "No hound is a match for me. I warned you. I will enjoy tearing all of you apart for an evening bite!" Clara felt her blood run cold. She looked around frantically for Riley and Argus, but they were nowhere to be seen.

The wolf appeared to back away and for a second Clara thought everything would be ok until she heard a terrifying guttural growling sound.

She realized then that the wolf had doubled backed in order to give herself more distance with which to run straight at her in attack. It would be a matter of moments before the wolf reached her, leapt up onto the rock and devoured her. Clara froze in vice-like fear. Fog closed in on her mind clouding her ability to think freely or act.

And then all at once, she was not alone. Clara's eyes were like saucers as she realized two colossal grey wolves were standing on either side of her. Both wolves simultaneously let out deafening howls. Emboldened, Clara howled her most frightful howl from every cell and every bone of her body. The attacking wolf, astonished by the sound and the appearance of the grey wolves, stopped in a sudden halt just before the rock.

One of the Greys bellowed, "You will leave this land! You will not harm our clan! We wish you no harm. We are all one, but this is and has always been our home. You do not belong here! You may not hunt here! Go and return to your own clan!"

Clara very slowly turned her head to look at the grey wolf on her left. "Riley," she whispered, "Riley, is that you?"

Madame Wolf bared her teeth and pawed the ground in front of her, but she knew she had lost. The grey wolves were the largest, most dominant of all wolves, and were to be respected. What angered her more was that she couldn't understand why the most magnificent of her kind had accepted this strange, little creature as their own.

Madame Wolf would never come to understand what happened that night under the light of the full moon, because she could only ever think of herself and occasionally of others just like her. She bowed her head, turned, and skulked away into the night.

The grey wolves howled again at the full moon, and with the threat truly over, Clara collapsed, nuzzling into their necks crying, "Riley! Argus! It is you! I knew it was you, and that you would come to my rescue!"

Argus spoke in a deep reassuring voice. "You rescued yourself, Clara, with your courage, and with your faith in us as true friends. In this enchanted land, we stood by you as our spirit animal, the Grey Wolf. Know that you are never all alone."

"And what is to become of Madame Wolf?" questioned Clara.

"Madame Wolf will wander for the rest of her days as a foe to all, and a friend to none."

"On that cheerful thought," chuckled Riley, "Let's play, Clara! Climb onto my back. This time we will not be walking! Hold on!"

And with that, they were all in the air flying off the rock into the night sky. They galloped at unimaginable speed for miles. Clara felt the wind whip through her hair and she 'whoooooped' for joy, reaching her hands up for just a second to the night sky. They stopped before a great lake with the full moon reflected, shimmering on its still surface. The wolves danced and played with Clara and she laughed until they were so exhausted, they could play no more. They sat down together on the grass looking up at the full moon.

"Could we stay like this forever, so that I can speak with you, Riley and Argus, and we can be free to gallop and play throughout the nights?"

"Clara, we do speak with you, just in a different way back home," Riley answered. "We are always near to run and play. This feeling of freedom rests in your soul, along with your strength, courage and vision. All you have to do is close your eyes, and call it forth."

Clara listened to the wolves, and she felt the meaning of their words. She closed her eyes once more and brought a hand to her heart. She imagined the big, beautiful, full moon in its splendor. "Thank you, dear moon, for shining your light on me tonight!"

Clara didn't have to open her eyes to know something amazing was happening. She heard it. The sound of a piano playing, as though the melody was all around her, above her and below at the same time.

It was the sound of *Claire de Lune* or 'Moonlight', by Claude Debussy. The notes of the piano floated and swirled through the night air, caressing the sky, touching the twinkling stars. The sound reminded her of soft rain falling on a serene lake. My namesake in French, thought Clara. Somewhere under the light of the full moon, she caught a vision of her father seated at his grand piano playing his beloved piece, just for her.

Tears started to fall down Clara's cheeks. She wept not from sadness or loneliness, but for the miracle of love and faith.

"Clara! Clara, Darling! Wake up! We really must be going!" Clara opened one eye to see Esmeralda standing over her in bright sunlight waving her arms about, her velvet pouch sparking different colours and jangling every which way.

Instantly realizing she had fallen asleep, Clara sprang up and said, "Was I dreaming? Did you see the wolves Riley and Argus?"

"Of course I see Riley and Argus, silly girl. They are right behind you!"

Clara spun around to see her two Irish wolfhounds lying in the grass, occasionally rolling from one side to another.

"Esmeralda, you don't understand!" Clara explained. "They were great big grey wolves and we ran for miles, and they saved me from a mean, nasty wolf and, there was a full moon with music and…"

"Clara! Really? Honestly! The stories! We don't have time for all that."

Esmeralda held out her velvet bag.

Clara slumped her shoulders and said, "You don't believe me?! I thought you…"

"Oh, fiddle-faddle," Esmeralda said with a smile and a wink. "Clara, I know! You have completed the Passage of the Diamond. Now, *come on, off we go* for our final journey, and you might just see just how far you have come."

THE SAPPHIRE AND THE BUTTERFLY

With great anticipation, Clara reached into the velvet bag and withdrew a blue stone the colour of the brightest blue sky and the clearest blue sea. It felt as if she could never tear her eyes away from its azure depths.

"You have chosen the sapphire Clara. The Passage of the Sapphire will teach you about transformation, or in other words, peace and wisdom and *amazebubbles* fun!"

Clara closed her eyes, right hand on her heart, left hand clasping the sapphire. To her own surprise, Clara thought of her home. Clara felt appreciation and happiness picturing Darlington Manor and the purple lilac tree. She was sitting beneath its bows, smelling its fragrant flowers and reading her favorite book. She felt the grass beneath her feet and the warmth of the sun on her face.

Clara was smiling widely when she opened her eyes to see enormous pulsating blue circles. The blue glow from the circles surrounded and enveloped everything around her.

"You are ready," nodded Esmeralda and she walked ahead

through the sapphire portal. Clara, Riley and Argus followed behind, stepping into the blue circles.

Together they entered another area of a woodland forest. As they made their way along the path, Clara marveled at the towering beech trees. The sun shone through here and there in the great temple of high branches and beech leaves. Everywhere birds chirped and twittered. Occasionally she heard the caw of a crow. They wandered by gurgling streams, wild flowers scattered along their banks bursting with color. The forest seemed to be bathed in purples and pinks and greens. Just when Clara thought she had seen every lovely flower that could ever grow in the deep wooded forest, they rounded the bend to discover...

"BLUEBELLS!" Clara exclaimed. "Blankets of bluebells everywhere!" A legion of delicate blue flowers covered the hills, swirling up and among and around the trees. Clara twirled around in delight. Riley and Argus were about to jump into the sea of blue flowers when they heard a strange sound...faint at first, a slight tinkling and chiming and as it grew louder, jingling and jangling!

"Esmeralda, do you hear that?!" Clara called out, with no response. "Of course not," Clara muttered to herself, "Trust the Passage of the Sapphire."

"Ok, Riley and Argus, what's happening here?" Clara caught her breath when she peered closer at the hill of bluebells and saw that the flowers were swinging and swaying like little bells. Clara called out to the wolfhounds, "Look! The bluebells! The bluebells ring for us!"

And then, all at once, rows and rows of the swinging, ringing bluebells leaned to the left or to the right in front of Clara.

"The bluebells are making a pathway for us," she said in amazement. Riley and Argus woofed in agreement. "It would be so much easier if you could talk," joked Clara.

Clara, Riley and Argus skipped and pranced following the trail, up and down the hills of chiming bells. With joy in her heart, Clara sang of bluebells from an old Scottish song,

"Oh where, oh where, tell me where does your highland laddie dwell? He dwells in bonnie Scotland where grows the sweet bluebells...and oh in my heart, I love my laddie well..."

They journeyed down another hill and the ringing bells began to fade as the path came to an end. Clara stopped cheery and weary, leaning on a massive fallen tree branch. She surveyed the valley below now painted in pastel hues of greens and shades of brown with long shadows cast by clusters of trees.

"Tadaaaa! Here I am!" Clara announced, "As the court of bluebells has heralded my arrival, I must be a very important person!"

"Important indeed," came a soft melodic voice.

Clara looked around eagerly. "I am very pleased to meet you, ahh, Miss, umm, but I can' t see you!"

"I am over here!" Clara stepped toward the sound of the voice. "Not there, here!"

Clara again moved in another direction. "No, no," came a gentle laugh. "Look up and out and you will see me." Clara was awestruck at the sight of a magnificent deep orange and brown-speckled winged Butterfly that fluttered delicately through the air in front of her, alighting on a white wild flower.

"Why Hello, Miss Butterfly! My name is Clara, and these are my friends Riley and Argus."

"Please follow me Clara, as we mustn't be late," said the

butterfly.

"Late for what, may I ask?" But Miss Butterfly was already up in the air and moving so quickly, Clara had to use all of her concentration just to keep her in sight and to stay on the footpath. They wound through the forest until they came upon an old wooden gate that opened onto a rolling green valley.

Clara lost track of Miss Butterfly as she fiddled and struggled with the wooden latch. She was about to call out for her when Clara heard the strangest sound.

"Teehee, heehee!" Clara stopped for a moment. "Is anyone there?" And she heard it again.

"Teehee, heehee," in a sort of low chortle. "Were you talking about meee?!"

Clara jumped back in surprise when a boy about her age and her height appeared in front of the gate with a very tall colorful turban atop his head. His skin was as brown as freshly plowed earth and his clear green eyes sparkled like Esmeralda's gems.

"May I help you, Lady Clara?" And in one swift movement, he unlatched the gate and swung it wide open.

"Well, I, thank you… err…Sir… ?"

"Sir Maheraj, at your service," he said with a bow and a flourish of his hand.

"I am here to escort you to the announcement and the very pronouncement of your arrival."

"Well that sounds very important. Thank you, Sir."

Sir Maheraj offered Clara his right arm. Clara stood up as tall as she could to prepare for her grand entrance.

He looked at her with a very grave expression, and said, "Let's do some cartwheels," and then belly laughed, "Ha hah hahahah haaaaa."

Clara was shocked and speechless for a moment, and then

she burst out laughing.

"Announcements and pronouncements are always so terribly serious don't you think?" said Sir Maheraj. "The older people get, the more serious they are about making announcements and pronouncements. The trick is to keep growing up without growing old. And that means cartwheels!"

Sir Maharaj threw his arms up in the air and twirled around sideways.

"Weeeeeeeeeeeeeeee!!!!!!!!!!"

"Sir, that's not a cartwheel," said Clara.

"Of course it is, Lady Clara. It's an upside down cartwheel. Just like upside down pineapple cake! Oh my!" he gasped. "The time is now!"

"What do you mean, the time is *now*?" questioned Clara.

"Don't you know?" asked Sir Maheraj, incredulous. "The time is always NOW! We must go IMMEDIATELY!"

With that, Sir Maheraj and Clara and the wolfhounds dashed up a hill, crested the top and were descending into the next valley, when Clara suddenly stopped in her tracks.

"Sir Maheraj, what is THAT?!" she said, pointing to the field below.

Sir Maheraj looked at Clara with a twinkle in his eyes, pursed his lips just so, showing off his cheekbones, and said, *"That*, Lady Clara, is for your arrival."

There, in a vast field, stood the most arresting wonder of a marquee. Its white cloth sides billowed in the wind and a sumptuous collection of white feathers swayed audaciously atop the dome of the marquee. The edges of the dome were boarded with deep blue braided rope. The front entrance panels were tied open with blue and golden ropes, weighty tassels hanging from their ends. Clara could see that inside, golden stars adorned the cloth walls and the domed ceiling. Low couches with velvet and satin pillows lined the starry walls. In the center of the marque stood a bamboo and wicker chair, made with a large rounded back and elegantly sloping arm rests.

"Are those giant moss elephants on either side of the marquee?" Clara asked in amazement. All at once, the green elephants were trumpeting in chorus! Sir Maheraj practically levitated a foot in the air.

"We mustn't be late! But wait. This just won't do!" he said, gesturing at Clara.

Sir Maheraj turned and reached somewhere, from where Clara couldn't tell, and presented her with a tiny velvet pillow. Resting on the pillow lay an exquisite tiara glimmering with sapphires and diamonds. Clara could barely breathe as she reached out to place it on her head. When she lifted the tiara off the velvet pillow, the sapphire drops danced among the diamond wildflowers and woodland birds.

Sir Maheraj escorted Clara to her chair in the center of the marquee. With a mischievous smile he looked at her and said,

"Lady Clara, is there anything else I can do for you?"

Without waiting for a response, he stepped out of the marquee, and like a grand conductor waved for the elephants to cease trumpeting.

Miss Butterfly landed gracefully on the armrest of Clara's chair. "There you are," she said, gently moving her wings. "I am pleased you have found your place."

"This truly IS magical, Miss Butterfly," gushed Clara. "But I don't belong here. I was joking when I declared that I am a very important person. I am just a girl, not a princess. This tiara doesn't belong to me."

"Did you know that I go through four stages of

development before I become a butterfly? It takes me a long time and consideration until one day I am ready to leave my cocoon. By the time I emerge as a butterfly, I feel joy with every beat of my wings and I fly free. You have made the journey to arrive here. This is your celebration, not as a princess, but as a woodland goddess! You are the goddess of the realm of your own creation. Know that you are powerful beyond measure. Enjoy it with love and lightness in your heart."

Miss Butterfly slowed the movement of her wings just long enough for Clara to see the letter C emblazoned in white on the back of one of her wings. Miss Butterfly fluttered up and away softly singing, "Enjoy, Clara. Enjoy!"

Before Clara had time to think another thought, she saw Esmeralda striding towards her.

"Now THIS is extraordinary! Sir Maheraj, I must say you have outdone yourself this time. You might have gone a *bit* far with the elephants. You woke every animal in all the valleys and forests!" she exclaimed with a "*ha!*" and a huge grin.

"I see you have met Sir Maheraj, Clara, my fellow traveler… the finest magical gem explorer in all the lands and the designer of dreams."

"Oh yes, he has been very kind."

"Well come on then, Sir Maheraj. It's time for our grand finale, is it not?!"

With a bow, Sir Maheraj turned, raised his hand, paused for a beat and began to trace curves downward and upward in the air. The whirling wind and the singing birds followed Sir Maheraj's conducting, working together to create some sort of ethereal woodland symphony. As the melody tapered off, with one dramatic gesture, Sir Maheraj signaled for a…

Crackle, hissss, whizz, BOOM!

Thousands of daisies in pinks and reds and whites whistled up into the air and erupted in fireworks, their petals raining down through the sky to the ground. Clara laughed and jumped up in joy, clapping at the dazzling site before her.

"Sir Maheraj, I dare say those were our finest daisy daylight fireworks yet," exclaimed Esmeralda. "And Clara, it seems you have most certainly found your sparkle and your wit!"
"The Passage of the Sapphire is almost complete. Clara, It's time to leave your tiara for safekeeping with Sir Maheraj and come with me." Esmeralda motioned for Clara and the wolfhounds to follow her.

Clara raced over to the Sir Maheraj to say good-bye. "Could we meet to play again?"

"Of course, Lady Clara! We are fellow travelers now, of miracles and magic!"

"How will I find you?"

"Oh don't you worry. I will know exactly where to find you, when you just close your eyes and remember all the things grown-old grown-ups never see, like upside down cartwheels, daisy fireworks and lily pad hopping. Until next time, Lady Clara."

Clara was about to ask him to accompany her a little while longer, when Sir Maheraj vanished, leaving behind a low, *"Tee heehee hee,"* floating in his wake.

RETURN TO DARLINGTON MANOR

Clara, Riley and Argus set off to look for Esmeralda and eventually found her reclining under an old, majestic weeping willow tree, its branches swaying gently with the wind. Esmeralda was so concentrated on the stream below the banks of the great willow, she barely noticed their arrival.

"Do you see something special in the stream?" asked Clara. Esmeralda turned to greet them excitedly.

"Special, indeed! Would you like to see for yourself, Clara?"

Clara lay down on her belly in the grass and leaned over the edge to see what magic lay before her in the stream.

She looked back at Esmeralda and pronounced, "I only see my reflection. There's nothing else here!"

"Look again and feel with your heart, Clara. And listen."

Clara leaned over the edge of the stream, resting her chin on her hands, and looked and waited. She felt a sense of melancholy, knowing her journey was coming to an end, and dread at the idea of going home.

Just then, she heard a familiar voice. Her own voice! Clara looked down at the stream, and to her surprise, her reflection was speaking!

Clara shook her head in confusion, and rubbed her eyes. She looked again. Her very own reflection was smiling and saying something. She sat up, and looked and leaned forward to listen more closely.

"I love you! You are enough! I love you! You are enough! I love you…"

Clara looked back at Esmeralda, questioning. "Clara, that is your soul speaking to you," she said.

Clara watched her reflection and listened and listened until she felt a sense of peace wash over her. It felt like warm fires and soft blankets. It felt like she would never be lonely and frightened again.

Clara stood up and hugged Esmeralda. Esmeralda hugged her back and said,

"The deepest love of all that lasts forever is the love that you give to yourself. Your love will shine out from your heart like a light that can never be dimmed. So be gone loneliness! You can return home now, knowing that everything you will ever need is right there inside of you. Your heart song, your courage, your vision and your purpose come from the love and light that is your essence. Oh silly me! How could I forget! There are also magic and miracles around every corner!"

Esmeralda unclasped her cape and draped it around Clara's shoulders. "I want you to have this. It will remind you of your power and of great adventures.

Follow the stream and it will lead you all the way home. Until we meet again…"

Esmeralda bowed her head ever so slightly, turned and walked away whistling, her velvet bag swinging, sparking and jingling as she went.

Clara set off in the direction of the winding stream with Riley and Argus. They walked and walked until the stream lead them up another hill flowing to an end into a natural spring.

Clara surveyed the valleys below, seeing her home in the distance. She looked up at the blue sky knowing that she was made up of that very sky, and of the sun and the moon and the stars. She opened her arms wide and up to the sky, her green cape flying behind her. She closed her eyes and called forth the grey wolves. They stood together as one.

Clara felt love, faith, strength and courage pulsating through her. She felt her destiny calling her.

"It's time to go home."

"Riley, Argus? How fast can we go this time?" Riley stretched his legs down and forward with a mischievous twinkle in his eye. Clara hopped onto his back.

As they galloped home over the fields, the sun reflected off a shimmering object in the distance. Just as they were about to reach the forest surrounding Darlington Manor, Clara thought she saw… was that the family car?

Clara, Riley and Argus slowed to a walk as they navigated their way in silence through the forest until they reached the grounds at the back of the Manor. Clara caught her breath when she saw her parents and the Ratsibor sisters standing together at the top of the steps next to the stone lions.

Clara's heart leapt for joy. She lingered for a moment, observing her Father leaning on a walking stick, bandages visible under his suit jacket and a long coat draped over his shoulders. Her diminutive Mother suddenly seemed a tower of strength as she stood facing the Ratsibor sisters. Clara could hear Mrs. Heart shouting,

"How *DARE* you leave Clara alone in the forest for so long with or without the wolfhounds! By the time I am through with you two, you will not know if you are coming or going. I will have you locked up for good!"

Riley spoke "Clara, this is as far as we can go as wolves." With a glint in her eye and a wicked grin, Clara said: "Well, shall we?!"

Clara drew in a deep breath and together she and Riley and Argus let out their most deafening howls:

"Awoooooooooooooooooooooo!"

There was a collective gasp, as the Ratsibor sisters and Mr. and Mrs. Heart looked around wildly for the source of the sudden frightening sound.

Clara, now followed by her two wolfhounds, came bounding out of the forest into the open, and ran towards her parents. Reaching her Father first, Clara flung her arms around him, almost knocking

Mr. Heart to the ground.

For just a moment, the Ratsibor sisters froze in fear, as Riley and Argus headed straight for them. *"RUNNNNN!"* yelled Lucinda. Lilith and Lucinda took off sprinting around the house and down the driveway as Riley and Argus ran them out of Darlington Manor for good.

In a moment Mrs. Heart had her arms wrapped around Clara and Mr. Heart, so that all Clara could feel were the warm embraces of both her Mother and her Father. "Clara, thank Heavens you are safe," whispered Mr. Heart.

Clara took a step back and looked up at her Mother and Father.

"I *am* brave and strong. I went on a great adventure, and I learned of miracles and that I am magical."

Mr. Heart didn't seem surprised in the least. "Lets go inside my brave Clara, and you can tell us everything about this great adventure. Perhaps we should start with how you came to possess this extraordinary green cape!"

Clara followed Mr. and Mrs. Heart up the staircase to Darlington Manor and paused hearing the distinct sound of the robin's song. Clara rested her hand on the mane of one of the stone lions, looked up at the afternoon sky and caught sight of the majestic eagle flying high above.

THE END

Imagine. Inspire. Transform. Words to live by for Author and Producer, Cavan Mahony.

Born and raised in Boston, Massachusetts, Cavan now resides in the English countryside with her husband, son, and their beloved dog, August.

A graduate of Wellesley College with an MBA from Harvard Business School, Cavan's own personal journey has been filled with twists and turns, miracles and magic.

Her entrepreneurial spirit led Cavan into the international world of luxury fashion and beauty, working with iconic houses including Lancôme, Chanel, and Missoni.

It was her passion for storytelling, self-discovery and transformation that inspired Cavan to write her first book, Clara and the Magic Circles, and to co-found Coat Company Productions, a UK-based media platform that seeks to inspire and entertain with authenticity.

Cavan has written "Clara and the Magic Circles" to encourage children to believe in their limitless potential and manifest their dreams.

Lightning Source UK Ltd.
Milton Keynes UK
UKHW020844290721
387912UK00005B/140/J